P9-CRK-853

Zeke Meeks
RUN! FROM BUFFY

Zeke Meeks is published by
Picture Window Books
A Capstone Imprint
1710 Roe Crest Drive
North Mankato, Minnesota 56003
www.capstonepub.com

SLOBBER SMOOCHER

Library of Congress Cataloging in Publication Data
Green, D. L. (Debra L.)
Zeke Meeks vs. the gruesome girls / by D.L. Green ; illustrated by Josh Alves.
p. cm. — (Zeke Meeks)
Summary: Third-grader Zeke Meeks already has two sisters, so he is bitterly disappointed when his new neighbor proves to be a girl—can Charlie change his mind and prove to him that boys and girls can play together?
ISBN 978-1-4048-6805-2 (library binding)
ISBN 978-1-4048-7221-9 (pbk.)
1. Friendship—Juvenile fiction. 2. Brothers and sisters—Juvenile fiction. 3. Gender identity—Juvenile fiction. 4. Schools—Juvenile fiction. [1. Friendship—Fiction. 2. Brothers and sisters—Fiction. 3. Schools—Fiction. 4. Humorous stories.] I. Alves, Josh, ill. II. Title. III. Title: Zeke Meeks versus the gruesome girls.

PZ7.G81926Ze 2012

813.6—dc23 2011029900

Vector Credits: Shutterstock
Book design by K. Fraser

Printed in the United States of America in Stevens Point, Wisconsin.
102011 006404WZS12

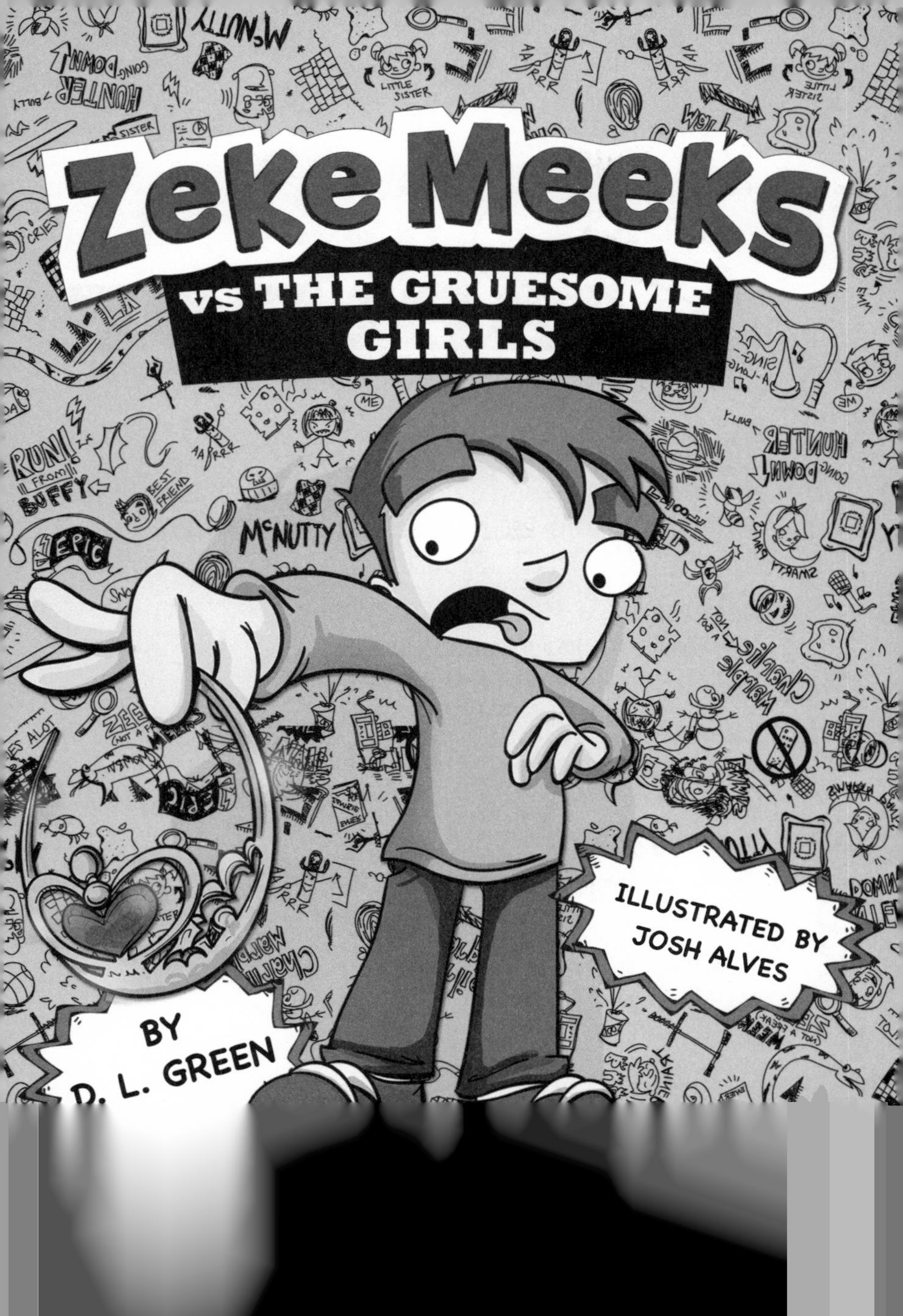
Zeke Meeks
vs THE GRUESOME GIRLS
ILLUSTRATED BY
JOSH ALVES
BY
D. L. GREEN

TABLE OF

GRACE CHANG's WICKED FINGERNAILS

CONTENTS

GIRLS DROOL ALL BUT GRACE – SHE BITES

Princess-crazy baby sister

SCREECHING, Shouting, Dancing Around

Ice Cubes

My sister was killing me. She wasn't shooting me, stabbing me, or poisoning me. But she was doing something almost as bad: She was hogging the TV. I wanted to watch a great show called *Fight, Fight, Fight*. But Mom said I had to wait for Mia's show to end.

Mia was watching *Princess Sing-Along*. It's the worst TV show ever, starring the worst princess ever, singing the worst songs ever. Yuck.

And Mia wasn't just watching the show. She was also screeching the songs out loud — really, really loud. She screeched, "When others are around, la la la, keep your noise level down, la la la."

"Listen to Princess Sing-Along," I told Mia.

"What?" she asked. Then she kept singing.

"Listen to Princess Sing-Along!" I shouted over Mia's screeching.

"I *am* listening to her," Mia said.

"Princess Sing-Along is telling you to keep the noise level down when others are around," I said.

"Yeah, I know!" Mia shouted. Then she screeched even louder, "When others are around, la la la, keep your noise level down, la la la."

"I'm around. So keep your noise level down," I said.

Mia shook her head. "You don't count, Zeke. You're my brother." Then she sang even louder, "When others are around, la la la, keep your noise level down, la la la."

"I can't stand the *Princess Sing-Along* show! I can't stand the princess! I can't stand the songs! And I really can't stand when you sing along with them!" I screamed.

Our mother ran into the room. She said, "Ezekiel Heathcliff Meeks, keep your noise level down. You're being much too loud."

I said, "Mia was the one who —"

"I heard you screaming, Zeke," my older sister, Alexa, interrupted me. She had come into the room with our dog, Waggles.

Waggles is a boy dog. But he was dressed like a girl dog. He wore a bright pink sweater around his big belly. He had a matching bright pink scarf around his neck. "Waggles looks girly," I complained.

"I put together a new outfit for him. Doesn't he look great?" Alexa said.

"Girly is great!" Mia said. Then she sang another Princess Sing-Along song. "Hearts and lace and flowers, la la la. Celebrate girl power, la la la."

"With Dad gone, there's too much girl power in this house," I said. I really missed my dad. He's a soldier. He was away on a top-secret mission.

Alexa patted my head. She said, "I know just the thing to cheer you up, Zeke. You should go to the mall. Try on some cute shoes. Look at the newest fashions. Shopping always makes me feel better."

"Yuck. That's a girl thing. That won't cheer me up," I said.

"I know how to cheer you up. We'll have a tea party," Mia said.

"That's a girl thing too," I said. I wished I had some guys around. I used to play a lot with my neighbor, Cole Kennedy. Cole was really funny. He liked to stick mini marshmallows up his nose and then eat them. He could make loud, stinky farts whenever he wanted. But he moved away last week.

The only other boy in the neighborhood was Hunter Down. He was older and much bigger than me. And he was a horrible bully.

"Zeke, I can cheer you up," Mom said.

I sighed. Mom was probably going to suggest a girly thing too, like going to the beauty salon for a lovely new haircut.

Mom said, "I can cheer you up with good news. We're getting new neighbors. A family is moving into Cole Kennedy's old house tomorrow. I heard they have a kid your age named Charlie."

"That *is* good news," I said.

"And I have more good news," Mom said. "In a few days, your dad will be home from his top-secret mission."

"That is *great* news!" I exclaimed.

"Also, it's supposed to start snowing tonight. Maybe it will snow so hard that the schools will be closed tomorrow for a snow day," Alexa said.

"Canceling school is always good news," I said.

It started snowing that night. I tried to do everything I could to get my school closed for a snow day tomorrow. My best friend, Hector Cruz, said that brushing your teeth with your left hand leads to a snow day.

Mom almost fell over from shock when she saw me brushing my teeth. I *never* brushed my teeth unless Mom reminded me, ordered me, or yelled at me. Often she had to remind me, order me, and yell at me. But that night, I brushed my teeth on my own.

My classmate Owen Leach thought the best way to get a snow day was to wear pajamas inside-out and backward. So I put on my pajamas without Mom's reminder, order, or yell.

That shocked Mom so much that she really did fall over.

Then I tried something my old neighbor Cole used to do to get a snow day. I put six ice cubes into a bowl. Then I put the bowl on the kitchen floor and danced around it.

My sister Alexa walked into the kitchen. She took one look at me and said,

I said, "I'm doing a special dance to get a snow day at my school."

"That's dorky," Alexa said. "Also, your pajamas are inside-out and backwards. They look dorky, too."

I stuck out my tongue at her.

"Sticking out your tongue is dorky, too. Also, it's gross," she said.

I grabbed the bowl of ice cubes, walked into the bathroom, and flushed the ice cubes down the toilet. My friend Danny Ford said that flushing ice cubes down the toilet was the best way to get a snow day.

My sister Mia stood outside the bathroom door. She screeched a Princess Sing-Along song. "Don't waste good water from the sea, la la la. Flush toilets just for poo and pee, la la la."

I closed the bathroom door and shouted, "Mind your own business!"

She shouted back, "Toilets *are* my business!"

Then Mom shouted, "Zeke, don't shout! And it's bedtime."

I shouted, "Mia was shouting, too."

Mom said, "Mia's just a little girl. You should know better."

I was so tired of my mom and sisters. I couldn't wait until my dad came home.

I went to the kitchen, took out a spoon, and licked it. Then I went to my room and put the spoon under my pillow. Rudy Morse had said that was sure to bring about a snow day.

I had great dreams that night. First I dreamed that my school was closed for snow days all week long.

Then I dreamed that I lived on a planet made out of candy. Cole and my friends from school lived there, too. We watched TV, played basketball, and ate candy all day. Girls were allowed on the planet only on Saturday mornings and one Tuesday a month.

Sure, they were weird dreams. But they were very happy ones. I wished they'd come true.

YEP.
I DEFINITELY
Have a
Problem
with
GIRLS

My radio alarm clock went off the next morning. But I stayed in bed. The radio DJ listed all the schools from A to Z that were closed for a snow day: Alistair Elementary, Arroyo Vista Elementary, Bob Barker Middle School. That was my sister Alexa's school. It would be a while before the DJ got to the Ws. My school was Worthsome Elementary.

I looked out my window. It was snowing. I was sure my school would be closed today.

I planned to watch TV, play video games, work on my LEGO circus, and read my book about the world's fiercest animals. I would stay in my pajamas all day. It was going to be great.

Finally, the DJ got to the Ws. Washington High School was closed. Waxie Middle School was closed. Wilson Elementary School was closed. Xavier High was closed. And Ziggler Elementary was closed.

I hadn't heard the DJ say Worthsome Elementary. But it *had* to be closed. I probably hadn't been listening closely. Or maybe the DJ skipped it by accident.

I was hungry. I decided to start off my day at home with a big bowl of Choco Chunk cereal. I got out of bed, walked out of my room, and headed for the kitchen.

My mom, Alexa, and Waggles were in the living room. Mom was on the computer, Alexa was watching TV, and Waggles was sitting next to Alexa. He wore a silly, sparkly yellow bow on his head.

The TV show announcer said, "Welcome back to *The Top Twenty Most Kissable Teen Stars* show. We're at number nine, Romeo Rockman. Just looking at his juicy red lips will make you want to kiss them."

"Eww," I said. "Looking at Romeo Rockman's lips wouldn't make me want to kiss them. I don't want to kiss juicy red lips or any other kinds of lips." Nicole Finkle and Buffy Maynard kept trying to kiss me at school. I didn't like it one bit.

Mom looked up from the computer. She said, "Zeke, hurry and get dressed. There's a lot of snow. It will take a long time to get to school today."

"But the schools are closed," I said.

"My school is closed," Alexa said.

Mom nodded. "Most of the schools have snow days. But your school is open, Zeke. I checked online."

"Noooo!" I cried.

"Yes," Mom said.

“Ha, ha. Too bad for you,” Alexa said. Then she pointed to the TV and said, “Ooh, Romeo Rockman is so kissable.” She puckered her lips.

Waggles gave Alexa’s lips a big, slobbery lick.

“Eww,” Alexa said. She ran to the kitchen sink and washed her face.

“Ha, ha. Too bad for you,” I said.

Then Mom said, “Get ready for school, Zeke.”

"Ha, ha. Too bad for you," Alexa said.

I sighed.

Almost everyone at school was mad that we didn't get a snow day. Chandler Fitzgerald stood in the middle of the playground and cried about it. Chandler Fitzgerald cried about everything. He cried when the toilet clogged, when the tip of his pencil broke off, and when he used up all his tissues. I told him:

When I told him that I hoped his tears didn't freeze on his face, it just made him cry harder.

Victoria Crow said, "I'm glad we didn't get a snow day. I love school. It's easy for me. That's because I'm the smartest kid in third grade."

Laurie Schneider threw a snowball at her.

That was the only good thing that happened that day at school.

At lunchtime, it was too cold to go outside. Our teacher, Mr. McNutty, said he'd show us a movie.

"Can you show us *Battle of the Cougars and Lions*?" I asked. He shook his head.

"How about the movie with the helicopter chasing the race cars around the football stadium?" Owen Leach asked.

Mr. McNutty shook his head.

"Let's watch *The Boy Who Couldn't Stop Farting,*" Rudy Morse said.

Mr. McNutty shook his head again. Then he closed the window shades, turned off the lights, and started the movie.

It was called *Serena's Beautiful Ballet Dream*. It was about a girl named Serena who dreamed of being in a beautiful ballet. Yuck.

For a few minutes, I watched the girl dancers doing girly twirls with girly tutus and girly ribbons. Then I closed my eyes. I was so tired of girls and their girl stuff.

Suddenly, I felt something gross and wet on each of my cheeks. I also heard disgusting slurping noises.

"I hear disgusting slurping noises," Mr. McNutty said. He turned the lights back on.

I saw where the gross wet things on my cheeks and the disgusting slurping noises had come from. Nicole Finkle was crouched on my left side. Buffy Maynard was crouched on my right side. They were both kissing me.

"Yuck!" I screamed. I rubbed my cheeks with the back of my hands, trying to get rid of the kiss marks.

The whole class laughed.

Mr. McNutty said, "Nicole and Buffy, you will have to stay inside during recess all week."

"If it keeps snowing, we'd have to stay inside all week anyway," Nicole said.

"And kissing Zeke Meeks was worth it," Buffy said.

"Yuck. No it wasn't," I said.

I was entirely, totally, wholly, utterly, and completely sick of girls.

SHAKERS
MOVING
Sorry
About
CHARLIE

I was very glad when school finally ended and Mom came to drive me home.

I was not glad when my little sister Mia started singing in the minivan. She screeched a Princess Sing-Along song. "Yellow snow that's in the street, la la la, is not something you should eat, la la la." Then she asked, "How does snow turn yellow?"

"It gets peed on," I said.

"Eww," she said.

Then she sang the yellow snow song again. And again. And again and again and again.

I covered my ears most of the way home.

Mom pointed to a moving van that was parked across the street at Cole's old house. "The new neighbors are moving in," Mom said.

I couldn't wait to meet Charlie. I hoped he liked video games and basketball. "Can I go over there and welcome Charlie to the neighborhood?" I asked.

"Charlie's family is probably very busy now. Wait until the moving van leaves," Mom said.

I made a snowman in our front yard. Cole and I used to make all kinds of snowmen. We had made a pirate snowman with an eye patch and a hook. We made a vampire snowman with a cape, fangs, and fake blood that was really fruit punch.

My favorite was a monster snowman with half a head, three eyes, and one arm. Today, I just made a regular snowman. It wasn't much fun doing it by myself.

My sister Alexa came outside. She said, "That snowman is boring. I'll help you make it better."

"Okay. Maybe we could give it a hunchback or a horn coming out of its neck," I said.

"I have a better idea," Alexa said. She took a purple flowery hat and a purple beaded necklace from her purse. Then she put them on my snowman — even the purse!

"Why do you have to make everything girly?" I asked.

"Girly is good," Alexa said.

"I'm so sick of girly stuff," I said.

She shrugged and returned to the house.

"Hey! You left the girly stuff on my snowman!" I yelled. But Alexa was already inside.

Then the moving van pulled away. I carefully crossed the street and knocked on the new neighbors' door. A man answered.

I said, "Hi, I'm Zeke Meeks. I live across the street."

"Nice to meet you," he said with a smile.

"Nice to meet you, too. I was wondering if Charlie wants to play," I said.

The man said, "Hold on. I'll check." Then he turned toward the house and called, "Charlie! A boy who lives across the street wants to play with you."

A girl my age quickly came to the door. "Hi," she said.

"Hi. Is your brother home?" I asked.

"I don't have a brother," she said.

"Well, is Charlie home?" I asked.

"I'm Charlie," she said.

Oh, no. Charlie was a girl. Yuck. I already had too many girls in my life. My yucky sisters and yucky mom and all the yucky girls in my class were enough. I did not want another yucky girl in my life.

"What do you want to play?" Charlie asked.

I sure didn't want to play dolls or dress-up or any other girl thing. I took a step back and said, "I forgot I have something to do."

"What do you have to do?"

"Bye," I said. Then I ran away.

"You jerk!" she screamed. "You don't have anything to do! You just don't want to play with me!"

I kept running toward my house.

Then I tripped over something. I fell into a mound of snow. Above me stood Hunter Down, the bully of my neighborhood. The something I had tripped over was Hunter Down's foot. Hunter's foot is huge and strong. So is everything else of Hunter's, except his brain and his heart. His brain and his heart are puny and weak.

Hunter threw a snowball at me. Then he laughed and walked away.

I lay in the snow, thinking that things could not get any worse.

Then I noticed the color of the snow: yellow.

Things had gotten worse.

Just as I stood up, another snowball whizzed by. It knocked the purple hat off my snowman. I was glad about that.

Then another snowball whizzed by. It knocked me down again. I was not glad about that.

I got up and looked around to see who was throwing the snowballs.

Charlie stood across the street with a snowball in her hand. She had a good throwing arm. For a girl, anyway. I wondered if she played base—

A big, wet snowball interrupted my thoughts by hitting my face. I quickly made my own snowball. I threw it at Charlie.

It missed.

Then she threw another snowball at me. It hit my stomach and knocked me on my butt. She started screaming at me.

"I didn't know you were a girl when I asked. I don't play with girls!" I screamed back.

She threw a snowball at my shoulder. Then she ran across her front yard. She was a fast runner. For a girl, anyway.

She went inside a snow fort. I hadn't seen it before. She must have made it today. It was tall and wide and had a window. Charlie was a good fort builder. For a girl, anyway.

I made sure no cars were on the road. Then I rushed toward Charlie's snow fort. Once I got near it, I bent down to make a snowball.

Then she beaned me with another snowball. It landed on my chest and made me spin around.

Then things got even worse.

A big, long, gray thing flew near my face. I guessed it was a gigantic insect.

I am terrified of insects. I am even more terrified of gigantic insects. I raced back to my house as fast as I could.

Charlie shouted, “What a scaredy-cat!”

I couldn’t stand that girl. From now on, I would stay far, far away from her. But that might be hard. She did live across the street from me.

She screamed, “I should tell everyone in your class what a scaredy-cat you are!”

"You don't even know anyone in my class!" I screamed back.

"I will soon. I'll be in your class tomorrow."

Things had gotten even worse.

I shouted, "I'm not a scaredy-cat!"

"Then why did you just run away?" she asked.

"Because there was a huge creature flying at me," I said.

"That was a little feather."

"Oh," I said.

"Scaredy-cat!" Charlie shouted.

"I'm not a scaredy-cat!" I shouted again.

Then I rushed into my house, slammed the door, and threw myself under the coffee table.

CHARLIE and the Face RIPPER-OFFER

The next morning, I lay in bed worrying about Charlie. What if she told everyone at school that I was a scaredy-cat? What if she threw more snowballs at me? What if she and Hunter Down got together and beat me up?

I was driving myself crazy. I told myself not to think about Charlie. I still had an hour before I'd see her at school.

I was wrong. When I got into the minivan, Mom said, "We're going to carpool to school with Charlie's family."

I scowled.

Charlie sat in the back row of the minivan, right next to me. She scowled, too.

Charlie's little sister sat in the middle row, next to my sister Mia. She said, "Hello. My name is Max."

"I know a boy named Max," Mia said.

"Well, I'm a girl. Max is short for Maxine," Max said.

"Oh, cool," Mia said. "I won't scowl like my brother."

I scowled again.

"And I won't scowl like my sister," Max said.

Charlie scowled again, too.

Mia sang, "It's okay if you feel sad, la la la."

Max said, "Hey, that's a Princess Sing-Along song. I love Princess Sing-Along."

Mia clapped her hands and said, "Yay! Let's sing together."

Then they both screeched, "It's okay if you feel sad, la la la. But it's more fun to be glad, la la la."

“I’m not sad. I’m mad,” I whispered to Charlie.

“I’m madder,” she whispered back.

“Well, I’m furious,” I hissed.

“Well, I’m furiouser,” she hissed back.

“Furiouser isn’t even a word,” I said.

“I’m so furious that I had to create the word furiouser to show just how furious I am,” she said.

“Well, I’m more furiouser than you. I’m furiousest,” I said.

She scowled.

I scowled back at her.

As soon as my mom dropped us off at school, I rushed over to my friends.

Charlie stood on the playground by herself. Even though I was furiousest at her, I felt a little sorry for her.

When school started, our teacher, Mr. McNutty, said, "Class, please welcome Charlie Marple. She just moved here. Charlie, sit next to Grace Chang. It's the only empty seat."

The seat had been empty for a reason. No one wanted to sit next to Grace Chang. Believe me, she was evil. She dressed in girly dresses and she was short and thin. So she looked sweet. Adults thought she was sweet. But she was not at all sweet.

She was evil — pure evil. She had long, sharp, and evil fingernails. She used them as evil weapons for her evilness.

"Where did I put that math handout?" Mr. McNutty mumbled. He crouched behind his desk, opening and closing drawers.

While Mr. McNutty was crouched behind his desk, Grace talked to Charlie in a soft but evil voice. She said, "If you annoy me, I'll rip your face off. I'm serious."

Now do you believe me that she was evil?

Emma G., who sat behind Grace, said, "Yeah. She's serious about ripping your face off."

Emma J., who sat behind Emma G., said, "Yeah. She's serious about ripping your face off."

Yeah. She really was serious.

Grace threatened to rip people's faces off a lot. It was very scary. I didn't actually know anyone who had gotten their face ripped off.

But I'd heard stories about it. I heard that Grace had left kids with only half a face, or no forehead, or just a nose.

"If you try to rip my face off, I will grab your fingers and rip your nails off, one by one," Charlie said.

My mouth opened wide. No one had ever threatened Grace before. Charlie was brave. For a girl, anyway.

I looked around the room. Everyone except Charlie had their mouths open wide. Grace's mouth was open the widest. Meanwhile, Mr. McNutty finally found the math handouts and stood up.

Then he asked, "Why does everyone except Charlie have their mouths open wide? Especially Grace's mouth. Her mouth is open so wide, I can see all her teeth and her tonsils."

"Opening your mouth wide is the best way to taste tiny bits of sugar floating in the air," Charlie said.

"Really?" Mr. McNutty opened his mouth wide. Then he joked, "I think I just tasted a few bits of sugar. Thank you, Charlie."

I laughed. Charlie was funny. For a girl, anyway. I wondered if we could be friends.

Then I remembered that she had yelled at me, thrown snowballs at me, called me a scaredy-cat, scowled at me, and said I made her furiouser.

Charlie and I would never be friends. Never, ever, ever.

ME,
MYSELF,
and Hunter
DOWN

After school, I started building a snow fort. I wanted to attack Charlie with snowballs and then hide in the fort.

I had made forts before, with my dad, my old neighbor, Cole, and my best friend, Hector. But this was the first time I'd built one by myself. It was really hard. The fort came out a lot shorter and smaller than I'd planned. That's because I was a lot more tired and cold than I'd planned.

I made some big snowballs. Then I waited for Charlie to come out of her house. I didn't even know if she would. But I wanted to be prepared.

I waited a long time for her. Staying in the snow fort by myself sure was boring. If my dad were here, I'd have had someone to talk to. If Cole were in the fort, we'd probably have a burping contest. Cole's burps were louder, but I could do more of them. My record was 33 burps in one minute. If Hector were here, we'd probably tell each other jokes.

I decided to tell myself a joke. "Hey, Zeke," I said.

"What?" I asked myself.

"What kind of dog loves bubble baths?" I asked.

"A shampoodle. I know that one," I answered.

"Okay, here's another one. What did the idiot call his pet zebra?" I asked myself.

"Spot," I said. "I knew that one, too. Telling jokes to myself is boring."

"I agree. You're a wise person," I told myself.

"And handsome, too," I replied.

Then I heard someone coming out of my house. "Who's that?" I shouted.

Mia walked over to the snow fort and came in. She was holding her Princess Sing-Along doll. "It's Mia," she said.

"I know who you are," I said.

"Then why did you say 'Who's that?'" she asked.

I said, "Never mind. I'm glad you came by. Do you want to make snowballs with me?"

"No thanks," she said. She looked around. "This fort needs decorations. I'll cover the walls with pictures of flowers. It will look so pretty."

"I don't want it to look pretty," I said.

She shrugged. "Okay, then let's play house in here. Do you want to be the baby or the mommy?"

"Neither one. I don't want to play house," I said.

"We can use the fort for a tea party instead," Mia said. "I'll bring in my tea set and more of my dolls. Princess Sing-Along, Daisy Darling, Miss Giggles, and Lady Lovely would all love some sweet, warm tea."

I shook my head. "I built this fort for battles, not tea parties."

She asked, “Can I use your fort for a dollhouse?”

“No,” I said.

“That’s no fun. I’m leaving.” Mia walked out of the fort.

I was all alone again. I looked out the window to see if Charlie had come out of her house.

I saw someone walking toward me. It wasn’t Charlie. It was a boy. A big boy. A big, frowning boy. A big, frowning, mean boy. It was Hunter Down.

He stopped walking when he got to my fort.

I started shaking, and it wasn't from the cold.

Hunter smashed his arm against the fort's wall. Then he kicked the wall. Then he smashed and kicked the wall at the same time. Then he did it *again* and again and one more time.

Actually, two more times.

Actually, three more times.

And then again.

And then . . .

Well, you get the picture.

It's not a pretty picture.

After a while, Hunter stomped off.

I walked around the fort to see what Hunter had done to it. I saw that he'd destroyed a lot of it. On the bright side, he hadn't destroyed all of it.

On the other bright side, at least Hunter had attacked my fort and not me.

Then Hunter threw a huge snowball at me. It hit my head.

My head hurt too much to think of any more bright sides.

Better Than
SANTA
CLAUS

Guess who was waiting for me when I got home from school the next day? Here are five clues:

1. He's very big.

2. He's a hero.

3. He traveled a long way to get here.

4. He made the world a better place.

5. He brought presents.

I'll give you some time to think about it.

This . . .

Is . . .

Me, giving you time . . .

Ready? Take a guess.

Did you guess Santa Claus? That would be a smart guess. Santa Claus is a very big hero who travels a long way, makes the world a better place, and brings presents.

But that guess would be wrong. The person waiting for me after school made me even happier than Santa Claus could: my dad.

As soon as I saw him, I jumped into his arms.

He hugged me and said, "I missed you, too, Zeke."

"How was your top-secret mission? Did you kill a lot of bad guys?" I asked him.

"We had some brutal battles," he said.

"You're so tough and brave and strong! I'm really glad you're home," I said.

He wiped his eye.

That confused me. Dad was too tough and brave and strong to cry.

Then he wiped his other eye.

Maybe he just had some dust in his eyes.

Then a tear ran down his cheek.

I asked my dad, “Are you injured? Did your eyes get hurt from an enemy bomb?”

“No. My eyes are fine. I’m crying,” Dad said.

“But I thought you were tough and brave and strong,” I said, even more confused.

Dad ruffled my hair. “I can be tough, brave, and strong, and still cry.”

That confused me too. “Are you sad that you’re home?” I asked.

“No. I’m crying from happiness,” he said. Then he gave me another hug.

I wasn’t confused anymore.

Dad hugged everyone in our family.

After he hugged Waggles, he plugged his nose. He said,

Mom answered, "I took him for a walk today. He rolled around in rotten eggs that he found in a moldy sewer."

"That explains it," Dad said.

Then he opened up a suitcase and said, "I have presents for everyone."

He gave Mom a necklace with a heart on it and matching heart earrings.

"Don't you think these are the prettiest things ever?" Mom asked.

The only thing I thought was yuck. But I nodded to be polite.

Dad gave Alexa a wooden jewelry box with flowers carved into it. Inside the box was a bracelet with flowers on it.

Double yuck.

Mia got some dresses for her dolls.

Triple yuck.

Dad gave me a football. Waggles got a football dog toy.

"Yuck," Alexa said.

“A football is just what I wanted,” I said.

Waggles drooled all over his football. That was his way of saying it was just what he wanted, too.

Dad said, “I hear Alexa and Mia have been dressing up Waggles in girl’s clothes.”

“Poor Waggles has had to wear bright pink sweaters and sparkly bows and other girly stuff,” I said.

"But he looks so cute in them," Alexa said.

"Waggles is a boy dog," Dad and I said at the same time. Then we smiled at each other at the same time.

Then Dad gave Waggles a cool black jacket with a skull on it, like tough guys wear.

Waggles drooled his approval.

Dad's last gift was for me. He gave me a book called *Toilet Jokes for Kids*.

I tried to read the first joke out loud. But I kept laughing too hard to finish it. Finally, I was able to read the whole joke: "If four out of five people suffer from diarrhea, does that mean that one person enjoys it?" I asked. "Get it?" I laughed again.

Alexa and Mia and Mom didn't laugh at all. They frowned and said, "Yuck."

But Dad and I couldn't stop laughing.

I gave Dad another hug. It was great to have another guy around.

Today Is
NOT
MY THING

Charlie's dad drove the carpool to school the next day. Charlie and I both scowled in the backseat.

My sister Mia and Charlie's sister Max sat next to each other again. They started singing a Princess Sing-Along song right away. They screeched, "Don't let your teeth rot and fall out, la la la. Eat good food like alfalfa sprouts, la la la."

"Gross," Charlie and I both said at the same time.

"I'll make an alfalfa sprout casserole for dinner tonight," Charlie's dad said.

"Hooray for alfalfa sprouts!" Max shouted.

"Hooray for alfalfa sprouts!" Mia shouted.

"Gross," Charlie and I both said again.

"Let's sing the baby dolls and basketballs song," Mia said.

"Okay," Max said.

"Oh, no," Charlie and I both said at the same time.

Then Mia and Max screeched, "Boys can play with baby dolls, la la la. And girls can throw basketballs, la la la. Boys and girls can play together, la la la. Friendships are a special treasure, la la la."

I whispered to Charlie, "I'll never play with you."

"Fine. Play by yourself. Maybe that bully will knock down your fort again," she said.

"You saw that? Were you spying on me?" I asked.

She said, "I wasn't spying. I just happened to be looking out my window. If you had been nicer to me, I would have beat up that bully for you."

I shook my head.

"You're dumb," she said.

"At least I'm not a girl," I said.

"That's a dumb thing to say," she said.

I scowled at her again.

Once we got inside school, I went over to the boys group and Charlie walked over to the girls group.

Laurie Schneider was showing off her new dress. She told the girls, "My dress has seven ruffles. And the pockets are shaped like hearts."

"Ooh! Ahh!" Grace Chang exclaimed.

"Yeah. Ooh!" Emma G. exclaimed.

"Yeah. Ahh!" Emma J. exclaimed.

"Charlie, do you like my dress?" Laurie asked.

Charlie shrugged. “It’s not my thing.”

“Why isn’t it your thing?” Laurie asked.

“I don’t like wearing dresses. Kickball is my thing. And it’s hard to play kickball in a dress,” Charlie explained.

Grace Chang said, “Kickball is for boys.”

Then Emma G. said, “Yeah. Kickball is for boys.”

Then Emma J. said, "Yeah. Kickball is for boys."

"Charlie, you're not our thing," Grace Chang said.

"Yeah. You're not our thing," Emma G. said.

"Yeah. You're not our thing," Emma J. said.

I couldn't help feeling a little sorry for Charlie again.

Owen Leach asked, "Who wants to play kickball with me at recess?"

Owen was the most popular boy in third grade. So most of the boys said they wanted to play kickball with him.

"Charlie Marple likes kickball," I said.

"I love kickball," she said.

"Boys don't play with girls," Owen said.

So at recess, I played kickball with the boys.

The girls played hopscotch and jump rope on the other side of the playground.

Charlie kicked around a ball by herself.

I couldn't help it. I felt really sorry for her.

The Lesson of a
DUMB
Princess
Sing-Along Song

Dad was waiting for me when I got home from school. He said, “Zeke, did you make that snow fort in the front yard?”

I nodded. “I didn’t do a very good job. And then Hunter Down smashed the fort.”

“Do you want help making a better fort?” Dad asked.

“Sure,” I said. I was so happy to have another guy around.

Then Dad asked my mom and sisters to help.

"I don't know how to build a fort," Mia said.

"I'll show you how," Dad said.

"I don't want to break a nail," Alexa said.

"Don't worry. Your gloves will protect your nails," Dad said.

"I need to start making dinner," Mom said.

"I'll make dinner tonight," Dad said.

So everyone agreed to help build the fort.

First, we searched for large containers to make snow bricks. We looked all over the house. I chose a LEGO bucket. Mom took the recycling bin. Mia got out her biggest beach bucket.

Then we brought the containers and some shovels outside. We packed snow into the containers. When we turned them over, we had snow bricks. We stacked the bricks to make walls for the fort.

It was pretty easy with five people helping. Mom and Alexa were very fast brick makers. Mia figured out the best places for the fort windows. We quickly made a tall, strong snow fort.

"What are you planning to do in this fort?" Dad asked me.

I shrugged. I didn't want to tell him my plan: to attack Charlie with snowballs and then hide in the fort.

"We should go back in the house now," Dad said. "It's starting to get dark."

I looked across the street. Charlie was standing behind her window.

"Can I stay in here a little longer?" I asked.

"Just a little," Mom said.

After my family left, I thought about a lot of things. I thought that being in a fort by myself wasn't much fun. I thought that I didn't want to be alone again with Hunter Down. I also thought about Dad crying when he first came home. And I thought about Charlie's snowball-throwing skills and my mom and sisters' fort-building skills. That made me think that guys and girls weren't very different after all.

And that made me think about the dumb Princess Sing-Along song Mia and Max had screeched this morning. I tried not to think about it, but that dumb song got stuck in my brain. "Boys can play with baby dolls, la la la. And girls can throw basketballs, la la la. Boys and girls can play together, la la la. Friendships are a special treasure, la la la."

That dumb song played in my brain so much it gave me a headache. After about fourteen rounds of the song, I realized something: Even though the song was from a dumb TV show for little kids, it wasn't really dumb. It was actually pretty smart. Boys and girls can play together.

I put my arm through the fort window and waved at Charlie. Then I put my head through the window and yelled, "Come here!"

Charlie walked over to my fort. She was scowling and holding a big snowball. I looked at her and said:

"Huh? Isn't that a dumb Princess Sing-Along song?" she asked.

I felt my face get hot, even though it was cold outside. "Let's be friends," I said.

"I thought you didn't want to be friends with a girl," she said.

My face felt even hotter. I said, "I changed my mind about that. Sorry."

She put down the snowball, stepped inside the fort, and looked around. She said, "This is really cool."

"Thanks. It came out a lot better than the fort I made by myself," I said. Then there was a long silence. I wasn't used to talking to girls.

Well, I talked to my mom a lot. But mostly I said things like, “Can’t I just stay up half an hour later?” and “Why do I have to make my bed every morning when I’m just going to unmake it every night?” and “Owen Leach gets a bigger allowance than me.” I talked to my sisters a lot. But that mostly meant saying “Stop annoying me,” “I’ll tell on you,” and “You’re so ugly that if you threw a boomerang it wouldn’t come back.”

It was hard to talk to Charlie when I thought of her as a girl. So instead, I decided to think of her as a friend. I asked her, "Do you like video games?"

"I love video games," she said. "My favorite is *Total Nonstop Action*. It's really fun."

"I've been dying to play that," I said.

"Do you want to come over one day and play it with me?" she asked.

"Yeah. Thanks," I said.

"So you're not going to scowl at me anymore?" she asked.

"Only if you beat me at the video game," I said.

"I will," she said. Then she grinned.

"No you won't," I said. And I grinned back at her.

Things Get HAIRY
LIKE WAGGLES'S TAIL.

My dad drove everyone to school the next day.

Mia and Max sang a Princess Sing-Along song over and over. "If you have to pick your nose, la la la, don't get boogers on your clothes, la la la."

Charlie and I made up our own song. "Zeke and Charlie despise songs, la la la, screeched by Princess Sing-Along, la la la."

My sister Alexa screamed, "You're all driving me crazy!"

Dad sighed.

I said, "Do you know you've sighed twenty-three times since we got in the minivan? Charlie and I have been counting."

Dad sighed again.

"Twenty-four times now," Charlie said.

Dad said, "I thought fighting enemy soldiers was the hardest thing in the world. That was before I drove five kids to school."

When Dad dropped us off, he sighed again. That sigh sounded different than his other twenty-four sighs. It sounded like a sigh of relief.

Charlie and I walked onto the playground together.

Grace Chang yelled, "Eww! Look at Charlie's coat. It's brown. Brown is a boy color."

"Yeah. Brown is a boy color," Emma G. said.

"Yeah. Brown is a boy color," Emma J. said.

"My coat is pink. That's a girl color," Grace said.

"Yeah. It is," Emma G. said.

"Yeah. It is," Emma J. said.

"You should be careful, Grace. A pink coat like yours stains easily," Charlie said.

Then she threw a dirty snowball at her. Brown mud splattered all over Grace's pink coat.

Grace screamed, "I should throw a snowball right back at you! But I can't. I'm wearing new gloves and I don't want to get them dirty. Emma G. and Emma J., you do it."

So Emma G. and Emma J. threw snowballs at Charlie. But their aim was terrible. Instead of hitting Charlie, they hit Hector Cruz and me.

So Charlie, Hector, and I threw snowballs back at them.

Then Owen Leach yelled, "Snowball fight!"

Soon every kid on the playground except Grace was throwing snowballs.

We laughed and laughed. The last time we'd laughed so much was when Mr. McNutty had a hiccupping fit during the principal's speech at the school assembly. Even Chandler Fitzgerald, who usually cries, was laughing.

The only person who wasn't laughing was Grace. She was still mad. She screamed, "Charlie Marple, you ruined my coat! I'll get you back for—"

She stopped talking when my snowball flew into her mouth.

That got Grace even madder. She spit out the snowball and screamed, "I'm so mad now that I'm willing to soil my new gloves!" She made a snowball and threw it hard at me.

She also had terrible aim. Her snowball landed on the back of Mr. McNutty's head. It knocked his hairpiece into a muddy puddle and knocked him on his bottom.

Mr. McNutty said, "My hairpiece is in a muddy puddle of slush. My bald head is freezing. My bottom is soaking wet. And I haven't been this embarrassed since I had that hiccupping fit during the principal's speech at the school assembly."

"You think you have it bad?" Grace asked him. "My gloves got dirty."

Mr. McNutty picked up his hairpiece. It was wet and covered with twigs, pebbles, and mud. He said, "This is all your fault, Grace. You will take my hairpiece home today. You will shampoo and comb it. Make sure you part it on the left side. Bring it back to me tomorrow morning."

"Yuck," Grace said.

I put my hand over my mouth to hide my laughter.

My classmates had their hands over their mouths, too.

Mr. McNutty walked away.

"This hairpiece is disgusting," Grace said.

Everyone took their hands off their mouths and laughed.

Laurie Schneider said, "That snowball fight was really fun. It was great having boys and girls play together."

"Charlie started it," I said.

Owen Leach said, "Charlie, you have a strong throwing arm. You should play baseball with us."

"Okay," Charlie said.

"And kickball, too," I said.

"Can I play on your team, Charlie?" Owen asked.

"Sure," Charlie said. "As long as Zeke can be on my team, too."

"Charlie and I are friends. We want to stick together," I said.

Things Get SAPPY
GRAB A TISSUE BEFORE YOU
READ THE LAST CHAPTER OF
THIS BOOK. I'M WARNING YOU!

Dad drove the carpool again after school.

Charlie told him, “I might be a soldier when I grow up. Either a soldier, a pro football player, or a nurse.”

“If you work hard, you can be anything you want,” Dad said.

“I want to be a porcupine when I grow up,” Max said.

“Well, that might be tough,” Dad said.

"Do you like fighting bad guys, Mr. Meeks?" Charlie asked.

"No. It's better to work things out without fighting. I'd rather have peace," Dad said.

"That reminds me of a Princess Sing-Along song," Mia said.

"Oh, no," Charlie and I both said at the same time.

Mia screeched, "Act like a princess, la la la."

Max joined in the song: "Give hugs and kisses, la la la."

Charlie and I both groaned.

Charlie said, "Princess and kisses don't even really rhyme."

I said, "There's only one thing worse than hearing someone screech a Princess Sing-Along song. It's hearing two people screech a Princess Sing-Along song."

"Giving hugs and kisses sounds almost as boring as trying to work things out and make peace," Charlie said.

"Sometimes we can't work things out. Then we battle our enemies with all our might," Dad said.

"Cool!" Charlie exclaimed.

When we got home, Charlie and I hung out in my fort. I explained how my family had built it. Charlie gave me some tips for making great snowballs. She told me to use snow from the warmest area I could find, dig a few inches down for it, and warm it a little with my gloves.

"Do you hear something?" I asked her.

We stopped talking and listened. Slow, heavy footsteps came toward us.

I peeked out the window of the fort. In front of me was the large, angry face of Hunter Down.

I whispered to Charlie, "Oh, no. Hunter Down is here. He's the biggest and meanest bully in the neighborhood."

Hunter shouted, "I heard that! I'm not a big, mean bully! But because you called me that, I'm going to beat you up!" Then he scratched his head and said, "Hey, I thought I destroyed this fort a few days ago."

"I made a better one," I said.

"His father helped him. His father is a huge and very strong soldier. You don't want to upset Zeke's father," Charlie said.

Hunter glared at her. He asked,

"I'm Charlie Marple. I'm your new neighbor," she said.

"After I beat you up and destroy this fort, you'll be sorry you ever moved into my neighborhood," Hunter said.

"Let's try to work things out," I said. "My father, the huge and very strong soldier, said it's best to make peace."

Hunter kicked the wall of the fort.

"That's not what I meant by working things out," I said.

"We want to make peace," Charlie said.

"I'll make peas. I'll make pea soup out of your face!" Hunter shouted.

"Pea soup? That doesn't even make sense," Charlie said. "You could make bloody skin soup from a person's face, but not pea soup."

"Are you insulting me by saying I don't make sense?" Hunter shouted.

"Yes," Charlie said.

He grabbed the front of her jacket.

I had to help my friend. So I jumped on Hunter's back.

The three of us fell to the ground. Hunter tried to punch Charlie and me. We tried to get away. But we couldn't.

We all rolled in the snow. It probably wasn't a pretty sight. In fact, it probably was an ugly sight. I couldn't see what kind of sight it was. I was too scared to look.

Then I heard more footsteps. They were loud and fast. Someone was walking up to us. I opened my eyes. That someone was my dad. He stood above us. I exclaimed, "Dad!"

"Wow, your dad really is huge and strong. Is he really a soldier?" Hunter asked.

"Yes," Dad said. Then he yelled, "Freeze! That's an order."

We all froze.

I opened my eyes. I scratched an itch behind my ear. I gave Dad a little wave. But other than those things, I stayed perfectly frozen. Oh, I forgot. I also licked my lips, adjusted my mittens, and wiggled my feet. But I was pretty much frozen.

Dad pointed to Hunter and said, "Listen, punk. Stay away from Zeke and Charlie. Pick on someone your own size. Better yet, don't pick on anyone at all. Find a hobby to keep you busy instead. Knitting, perhaps."

"Knitting?" Hunter asked.

"Yes. I'm making a nice wool sweater with ruffled sleeves for my daughter," Dad said.

"Alexa or Mia?" I asked.

"Mia," Dad said. "Anyway, punk, if you ever even touch Zeke or Charlie again, I'll turn your face into bloody skin soup."

"I told you that you couldn't make pea soup out of a person's face," Charlie said.

Dad added, "Then I'll crush the rest of you and wrench out your—"

"Okay, okay. I got the message," Hunter said in a squeaky, scared voice. "I'll stay away from them."

"You didn't say 'sir,'" Dad said.

"Sir," Hunter said.

"Put both phrases together," Dad said.

"Sorry, sir, but I forgot what the first phrase was, sir," Hunter said.

"It's 'I'll stay away from them.' Them meaning Charlie and me," I explained.

Dad looked at his watch. He said, "Please hurry. I've got cookies baking in the oven."

"What kind?" I asked.

"Chocolate chip," Dad said.

"I'll stay away from Charlie and Zeke, sir," Hunter said.

"Good. Now fix this fine fort. Then get lost," Dad said.

"Yes, sir," Hunter said.

He fixed the fine fort.

Then he got lost.

Once Hunter was gone, Charlie said, "Thanks a lot for rescuing us, Mr. Meeks."

"I'm so glad you're home, Dad," I said.

“I’m so glad I’m home, too. I really missed you. And I missed your sisters and your mom. And Waggles, too.” Dad started sniffling. Then he wiped his eyes.

“Are you crying again?” I asked.

Then I started sniffling, too. Then I wiped my eyes, too.

"Just thinking about how much I love you makes me want to cry," Dad said.

"Just thinking about how much I love you makes me want to cry, too," I cried.

Charlie handed each of us tissues. She said, "Just thinking about you guys crying makes me want to throw up."

I laughed through my tears.

Then I threw a snowball at Charlie.

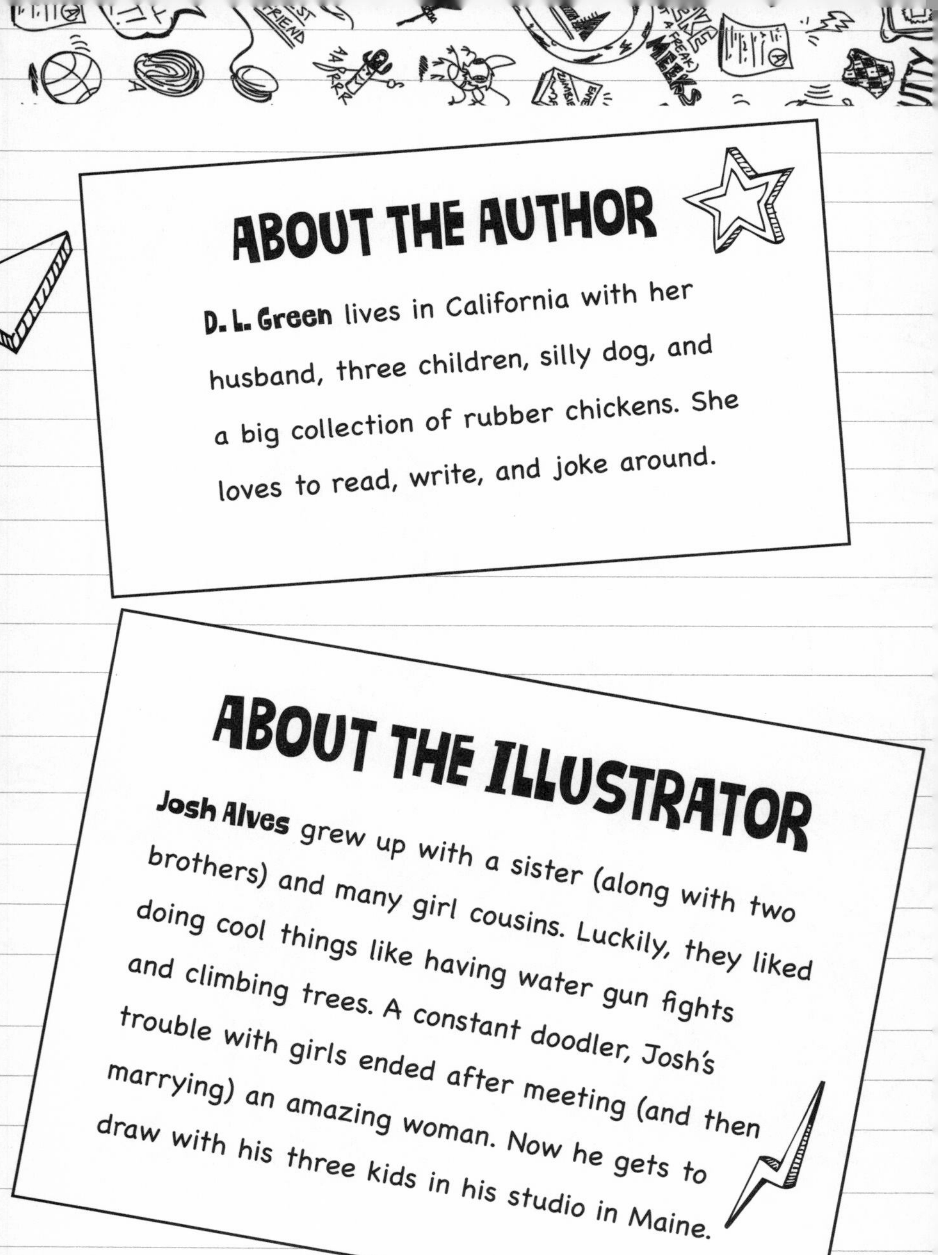

ABOUT THE AUTHOR

D. L. Green lives in California with her husband, three children, silly dog, and a big collection of rubber chickens. She loves to read, write, and joke around.

ABOUT THE ILLUSTRATOR

Josh Alves grew up with a sister (along with two brothers) and many girl cousins. Luckily, they liked doing cool things like having water gun fights and climbing trees. A constant doodler, Josh's trouble with girls ended after meeting (and then marrying) an amazing woman. Now he gets to draw with his three kids in his studio in Maine.

CAN GIRLS AND BOYS ACTUALLY BE FRIENDS?

(And other really important questions)

Write answers to these questions, or discuss them with your friends and classmates.

1. Can girls and boys actually be friends?

2. I learned some lessons about girls in this story. Can you guess what they were? Did you learn any lessons, too?

3. My whole family missed my dad when he was away. I despised being apart from him. Is there anyone you miss?

4. Do you think I dealt with Hunter Down the right way? What are your rules for dealing with bullies? Or are YOU a bully?!

BIG WORDS according to Zeke

TRY USING THEM IN SENTENCES JUST LIKE I DO

ANNOY: To completely and totally bug someone until they just about lose it.

APPROVAL: What you get when someone likes what you've done.

ASSEMBLY: A special event at school where the whole school comes together for a meeting or show or something.

DESPISE: To really, really, really, really, really hate something.

DIARRHEA: It's when you have to go to the bathroom a lot and what comes out is brown and watery. It is also SUPER gross.

DISGUSTING: Things that make you go "EW!" like love notes, most girls, and diarrhea.

FURIOUS: How you feel when someone breaks, loses, or takes something of yours. Also how you feel when a girl gets in your face.

GIGANTIC: Big, huge, large beyond belief.

LIKE VICTORIA CROW'S BRAIN. HUGE.

THESE COULD GET YOU INJURED IF HUNTER IS THE ONE THROWING THEM

INJURED: If you are injured, you have gotten hurt. When my dad was on his mission, I always worried about him getting injured.

SLOBBERY: Covered in spit from the mouth. Yuck.

SLURPING: A gross sound made when you suck up liquid with your mouth. Also the gross sound Nicole and Buffy made when they kissed me.

SNIFFLING: Something you do when you either (1) have a runny nose or (2) are trying not to cry.

THREATENED: When one person (like evil Grace Chang) told another person that he or she plans to do something horrible to them (like rip their face off). This is often done just to scare someone.

UTTERLY: Totally and completely, as in I am utterly scared of insects. (But don't tell anyone.)

WEAPONS: Things used to hurt another person or thing. Also Grace Chang's fingernails.

WWW.CAPSTONEKIDS.COM